The Fairy House

Fairy for a Day

Welcome to the Fairy House –
a whole new magical world...

Look for all *The Fairy House* books:

The Fairy House
Fairy for a Day

Kelly McKain
Illustrated by Nicola Slater

SCHOLASTIC

New York   Toronto   London   Auckland   Sydney
Mexico City   New Delhi   Hong Kong   Buenos Aires

ISBN 13: 978-0-545-04238-3
ISBN 10: 0-545-04238-0

12 11 10 9 8 7 6 5 4 3 2 1   7 8 9 10 11 12/0

Printed in China
First Scholastic U.S.A. printing, August 2007

For

Chloe and Gabrielle, with love

With thanks to

Amanda Punter, Katy Moran, Elaine McQuade, Andrew Biscomb, Georgia Lawe, Sarah Spedding, Kate Wilson, Claire Tagg, Eleanor Schramm, and Hilary Murray-Hill for working your magic on this, and for loving the Fairy House as much as I do! xx

Chapter 1

Katie skipped ahead of her mom all the way home from school, trying to get her to walk faster. As they turned the corner into the new housing development, she felt her heart leap with excitement. The houses were all the same, small and brown, like tiny Lego blocks — well, almost. Katie was proud that theirs stood out from the crowd. Katie's mom, an artist, loved all things bright and beautiful, so she'd painted the front door a vivid pink.

But it wasn't the house that Katie was excited about. She just couldn't wait to meet up with her four new friends. Once inside, she hurried through the living room and kitchen, dropping her book bag on the way. She was heading for the back door, but her mom made her sit down and have some orange juice and an apple first. Then she was gone, dashing across the yard and under the wire fence that separated their boring square patch of lawn from the over-grown, wild-flower-strewn almost-meadow that lay beyond. Katie swished through the tall grass, thick with dande-lions and daisies, humming a song that one of her new friends had taught her.

As she reached the oak tree and saw the dollhouse beneath it, she couldn't help smiling.

Although the dollhouse looked like any other, it certainly wasn't ordinary. Incredible as it sounded, Katie's new friends lived *inside* it — and they were *fairies*.

When Katie had first seen them, she'd hardly believed her eyes.

She'd left the dollhouse outside one night under the old oak tree, and when she returned the next morning she got a big

3

surprise! Four tiny fairies called Bluebell, Daisy, Rosehip, and Snowdrop had moved in!

Together, Katie and the fairies had transformed the pink plastic dollhouse into a beautiful home. Bluebell had decorated the walls with pressed-flower pictures, and there were rose-petal covers on the sofas and polka-dot curtains at the windows. They'd even made a string of tiny, sparkling fairy lights to keep the house cheerful at night.

Then Katie had painted the words "The Fairy House" on the front door in lovely swirly letters and given it to the fairies for their very own. Luckily, Katie's mom had allowed her to keep it under the oak tree in the almost-meadow.

Katie loved the way the Fairy House was becoming part of the landscape,

with Snowdrop's wonderful window boxes overflowing with pink and purple flowers, and the grass growing taller around the Fairy House as time passed.

Daisy and Snowdrop popped their heads out of Bluebell's bedroom window and waved to Katie. "Hurray! You're back!" Daisy cried.

"Come on in!" added Snowdrop. "You'll have to shrink first, of course!"

Katie grinned at them — she was really looking forward to more fairy fun! She crouched down beside the Fairy House and touched the tip of her little finger to the tiny blue door handle, which Bluebell had bewitched with fairy dust.

"I believe in fairies, I believe in fairies, I believe in fairies," she whispered. She gasped in delight as the top of her head tingled. Then a great

whooshing sound roared in her ears and everything around her seemed to be getting bigger and bigger and bigger. But, of course, she was getting smaller and smaller and smaller. And suddenly she was fairy-sized!

Just as she was about to go inside, Bluebell and Rosehip came whizzing around the oak tree. Bluebell was in the lead, with Rosehip right behind her, reaching out to touch her foot.

6

Bluebell spotted Katie, and just as she slowed a little to wave, Rosehip tagged her ankle. "It!" she cried triumphantly.

"That wasn't fair!" shouted Bluebell, hovering in midair with her hands on her hips. "I only slowed down to say hello to Katie!"

Rosehip tossed her fiery-orange hair and flew a few quick circles around Bluebell. "We were still playing so it *does* count, actually," she cried. "You're it! Ha, ha!" And with that, she zoomed past Bluebell, sticking out her tongue.

Bluebell lunged at Rosehip and Katie laughed as the two fairies became a shrieking ball of fluttering wings and flailing legs. They were the best of friends, but they also had hot tempers and were always getting into fights!

Just then, Daisy and Snowdrop rushed out of the door and grabbed Katie in a big hug. Bluebell and Rosehip came crashing to the ground, leaped up, and brushed themselves off, the squabble forgotten. All smiles, they joined in the hug.

"We made a jump rope with woven grass," Snowdrop said, pulling a long rope from the pocket of her skirt for Katie to see. "Will you play with us?"

"Of course," said Katie, "but first I have to tell you something — something very important. It's about your fairy task."

As soon as Katie said this, Snowdrop reached into the pocket of her dress again and pulled out the scroll they'd been given by the Fairy Queen herself. It said:

Fairy Task No. 45826

By Royal Command of the Fairy Queen

Terrible news has reached Fairyland. As you
know, the Magic Oak is the gateway between
Fairyland and the human world. The sparkling
whirlwind can only drop fairies off *here*.
Humans plan to knock down our special tree
and build a house on the land. If this happens,
fairies will no longer be able to come and help
people and the environment. You must stop
them from doing this terrible thing and make
sure that the tree is protected for the future.
Only then will you be allowed back into
Fairyland.

By order of Her Eternal Majesty

The Fairy Queen

P.S. You will need one each of the twelve
birthstones to work the magic that will save
the tree — but hurry, there's not much time!

Katie had been given a ring by her Aunt Jane, which turned out to be garnet, the January stone. So they'd found one, but they still needed eleven others. Katie had gotten a book out of the library and read up on the twelve birthstones. Some of them were very expensive, like ruby, sapphire, and emerald, and she had no idea how they'd get their hands on those gems.

"I found out from Mom that the man who built our house and this whole development is named Max Towner," Katie explained. "I bet he's the one who's planning to knock down the tree! And there's a girl named Tiffany Towner in my class, who's *really* mean and always getting into trouble. Mom said she's his daughter." The fairies all looked impressed with what Katie had found out. "The problem is that

Tiffany won't talk to me, because she thinks I'm a goody-goody," Katie continued. "I wanted to ask about her dad's plans, so I sat with her at lunch today, but she just ignored me."

"There is another way we could find out about Tiffany's father's plans," Daisy said slowly, a thoughtful look on her face. "One of *us* could make friends with her."

Katie stared at her, astonished.

"But how?"

"By turning big and going to school instead of you!" said Bluebell excitedly.

"We could say that

our family might be moving to town and that she's just visiting so no one would be suspicious," added Snowdrop.

"What a great idea!" cried Katie. "But how do you turn big? Do you just use a sprinkling of fairy dust?"

FAIRY DUST

There was a silence.

"Well?" Katie prompted. She realized that the fairies were all glancing at each other nervously from under their long eyelashes.

"Uh, not exactly *just* a sprinkling of fairy dust," said Daisy reluctantly, fiddling with her long braids. "There is a price to pay. For a fairy

12

to become a human, a human has to become a fairy, to take her place."

"You mean *me*?" Katie gasped, eyes gleaming with excitement.

"It takes courage," Daisy warned. "If something happened to one of you, the other would be stuck the wrong size forever. Or if one of you didn't want to turn back afterward, the other one couldn't. It's not something to be taken lightly."

All the fairies looked hopefully up at Katie, who stood perfectly still, feeling stunned. It was riskier than she'd thought — what if she got stuck as a fairy? She'd miss school, and Aunt Jane, and, worst of all, her mom would never see her again! She couldn't even *begin* to imagine how awful that would be!

But then she remembered the fairies' task, and how she'd promised to

help them in any way she could. If the tree were knocked down, it would be a disaster for Earth as well as Fairyland. Fairies looked after the seasons and all the plants, trees, and flowers. Without them, there might be snow in June, or maybe constant rain, or perhaps the fruit and vegetables wouldn't grow and there would be nothing to eat. She could only imagine what the consequences would be — but one thing was certain, they wouldn't be good! Katie took a deep breath and stood up. "We have to find out if Max Towner is behind this plan to knock down the tree," she said, "and this is the best chance we have. I'll do it."

"Oh, Katie, thanks!" cried Daisy.

"Well done!" added Snowdrop.

Bluebell suddenly stood up. "I'll do it, too," she announced, and they

all whirled around to stare at her. But no one said thank you or well done this time. In fact, no one said anything!

"What's the matter?" asked Bluebell.

"Don't take this the wrong way," said Daisy finally, in her gentlest voice, "but you'll never be able to stay calm with Tiffany. What if she says mean things about Katie?"

"I'll control my temper," Bluebell promised. "As Katie said, we have to find out if Tiffany's dad is behind these wicked plans, and quickly. Besides, it'll be fun, like being a secret agent and going undercover — I'll blend right in."

Katie giggled and clamped her hand over her mouth.

"What? What's so funny about that?" Bluebell demanded.

"You won't blend in with that blue hair!" Katie told her. "But if you're sure you can handle Tiffany, I'm willing to switch with you. You're very brave, Bluebell."

Bluebell did a happy twirl and finished it off with a curtsey.

"I was going to volunteer, too," Rosehip grumbled.

"Bluebell offered first, so it's only fair that she should turn big," Daisy told her. "We'll all need to go to school anyway, to look after Katie while she's small."

"Still not fair," Rosehip huffed, but she didn't say anything more.

"So we agree," said Katie. "Tomorrow we swap places!" She lunged over to hug Bluebell and they had an excited jumping-up-and-down squealy hug and dance around together, which the others soon joined in, even Rosehip. While the risks worried her, Katie was incredibly excited about becoming a fairy, even just for one day!

"I have to go in for my dinner soon," she said breathlessly, when they finally broke apart. "But there's just enough time to try your new jump rope, Snowdrop."

Snowdrop beamed at her and unrolled the rope. Rosehip made up a special fairy jumping song which

she taught them all, and pretty soon, she and Katie were jumping together, chanting, "Flap your wings and stomp your feet, jump in, Bluebell, don't miss a beat!" as Bluebell jumped in, too.

The chant made Katie feel extra excited — after all, tomorrow she

would be flapping her own wings, not just singing about it! She'd be a *real* fairy!

Jumping rope was so much fun that Katie almost forgot the time, until her rumbling tummy reminded her. Worried that her mom would come out looking for her and she'd be

nowhere to be seen, she gave her fairy friends a quick good-bye hug.

For dinner they shared one of her mom's homemade pizzas. (Katie knew that her mom hid all kinds of vegetables under the cheese, but somehow it was still delicious!) Then after she helped with the dishes, Katie dug out her own jump rope and asked her mom to play with her. They tied one end to the door handle and took turns turning the rope for each other. Katie couldn't resist singing Rosehip's skipping song.

"What a nice song," Katie's mom remarked. "Where did you learn that?"

"Oh, my new friends sing it at, um, school," mumbled Katie.

Katie's mom beamed. "I'm so

glad you're settling in so well, darling," she said, and, grinning, she began to turn the rope faster and faster.

Katie giggled, feet flying. "Mom, stop it!" she cried, not meaning a word.

Katie felt bad for fibbing to her mom, even just a little tiny bit, but she had *tried* to tell her the truth about the fairies when she'd first met them. The problem was that, like most grown-ups, her mom didn't believe in fairies and couldn't see them, so she just thought Katie was talking about imaginary friends she'd invented!

Later that evening, Katie took her bath and did her reading as usual, and soon she was all snuggled up in bed. But she was just too excited to sleep!

Eventually she got up and crept over to her window. Squinting into the darkness, she could just make out the Fairy House, glowing with the daisy lights she'd helped to make. Although she couldn't see into its tiny windows, she had a feeling Bluebell was still awake, too, gazing out into the almost-meadow, looking forward to her big day.

Chapter 2

The next morning as her mom walked Katie to school, she had no idea that four little fairies were coming, too! They were flying along at Katie's shoulder, wings shimmering in the sunlight, eyes shining with excitement.

As they neared the school, the fairies took cover in the front pockets of Katie's book bag, with just their heads poking out.

When Bluebell spotted some girls jumping rope on the playground she cried out, "Wow, maybe I'll get to do that when I'm big. Big jump ropes look even more fun than fairy jump ropes!"

"I bet you won't!" said Rosehip, and Katie realized that she was still jealous of Bluebell getting to be big instead of her. She hoped it wouldn't spoil their exciting day.

Once Katie's mom said good-bye, Katie and the fairies hurried to the school locker room to do the swap.

Katie took off her school tie and tossed it on a bench. Then she put her bag down on the floor and the fairies flew out.

She was really nervous, with butterflies in her stomach and jelly for legs. From the queasy look on Bluebell's face, she wasn't feeling much better!

Katie sat on the bench next to Bluebell and tried to push her worries from her mind. Snowdrop pulled the bottle of fairy dust from her pocket and sprinkled a little on each of their hands. Squeezing their eyes shut, Katie and Bluebell touched palms. There was an instant zapping feeling, like a spark of lightning rushing between them, and then a loud POP!

Katie leaped up from the floor and found herself the same size as Snowdrop. She did a twirl and fluttered her wings. "It worked!" she cried. "I'm a *real* fairy!"

"And I'm a *real* girl!" Bluebell gasped.

Katie smiled up at her friend — and noticed that she was now the same height as Bluebell's ankle!

They had to hurry to class, but Katie couldn't resist trying to fly a bit. At first she thought she wouldn't know how to do it, but it turned out to be as simple as reaching for a glass of milk. She *wanted* to fly, so the wings just fluttered slightly and up she went! Even being just a couple of inches off the ground was scary, though. She realized that it would take a while before she was doing somersaults and acrobatics in the air like the others!

Then the bell rang, making them all jump. Snowdrop clamped her hands over her ears and made a face.

"We'd better go," Katie called up to Bluebell, "or you'll be late."

"I'm not being ordered around by bells!" Bluebell shouted back. She stamped her foot, making Katie and the fairies dive out of the way.

"Careful, Bluebell," shrieked Daisy in alarm.

"Oh, sorry!" cried Bluebell. "I

forgot how big I am! It's just that I hate bells. If someone wants me to do something they can come in here and ask me nicely!"

Katie groaned. "You've got a lot to learn about school, Bluebell!" she said. "You *have* to listen to the bells. Look, just do your best to fit in with the others and keep out of trouble, OK?"

"Don't worry," said Bluebell. "I'll be perfect, you'll see. They'll never guess that I'm any different from the other children." With that she took Katie's tie off the bench and proudly put it on. Katie decided not to mention that it was crooked — Bluebell was so excited to be going to school and she didn't want anything to spoil her friend's big day.

Then the other fairies leaped into

the book bag and helped Katie climb in, too.

"All aboard," cried Bluebell, swinging the bag onto her shoulder so enthusiastically they all screamed. Now that she was fairy-sized, it felt like a carnival ride to Katie!

They grew more and more excited as Bluebell walked down the corridor, with Katie giving directions from the pocket of her book bag. Then, "Good luck," she added, as they reached the classroom.

Bluebell smiled thanks at her, then they all ducked down. If some of the

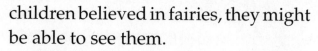

children believed in fairies, they might be able to see them.

When they were safely out of sight, Bluebell took a deep breath, crossed her fingers for luck, and opened the classroom door.

Chapter 3

Mrs. Borthwick, Katie's teacher, was a cheerful woman with a short gray bob, wearing thick tights and an orange dress. She'd been teaching so long that the oddest of odd things didn't usually surprise her, but even *she* was a little startled to see a complete stranger with a silky petal skirt, crooked school tie, and bright blue hair come marching through her classroom door.

"Hello, dear," she said kindly. "What can I do for you?"

When Bluebell explained that her family might be moving to town and that she was just visiting the school for the day, Mrs. Borthwick looked doubtful. But the little bit of fairy dust Snowdrop threw into the air around them soon made her believe it!

Blinking the fairy dust from her eyes, Mrs. Borthwick welcomed Bluebell to the class and asked her to take Katie's seat over by the window. The window was wide open to the June breeze. Bluebell sat down and propped a math book up against

the sill and the fairies climbed grate-fully out of the bag and hid behind it. They hated being cooped up, as Katie had found out when she'd tried to bring them into her house!

Bluebell didn't have to ask Katie who Tiffany was, because a whining voice called out, "Why doesn't *she* have to put her bag in the closet like everyone else, Mrs. Borthwick?"

Bluebell whirled around in her seat to see a girl with scraggly brown hair and a pink face giving her a mean stare.

"Now, Tiffany, Bluebell is our guest and she's only here for one day," said Mrs. Borthwick. "They probably have different rules at her school." She turned to Bluebell and smiled kindly. "Don't they, dear?"

Bluebell nodded. "Yes, we do. We keep all our things in our desks at

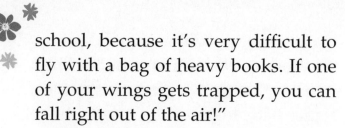

school, because it's very difficult to fly with a bag of heavy books. If one of your wings gets trapped, you can fall right out of the air!"

Mrs. Borthwick beamed at her. "How lovely that you like inventing stories, just like Katie!" she exclaimed.

"Oh, it's not a story," Bluebell insisted. "It's true."

Mrs. Borthwick raised her eyebrows. "Anyway, sit down, dear, and we'll all get on with the lesson," she said, a little sharply.

But Tiffany didn't want to get on with the lesson. Tiffany wanted to pick on Bluebell a bit more. "It's not fair that *she's* got blue hair!" she whined. "No one's allowed to dye their hair at *this* school!"

Furious, Bluebell leaped up from her seat and went crashing across

the classroom to Tiffany's desk. "It's not dyed, it's real!" she shouted.

"Liar, liar! Pants on fire!" chanted Tiffany, with a nasty sneer on her face.

"Bluebell, sit down at once," ordered Mrs. Borthwick, her usual cheery tone gone.

Bluebell stamped back to her desk but she couldn't resist twisting around in her seat to stick her tongue out at Tiffany. Katie poked her head out from behind the math book. She tried to cover herself by holding a piece of graph paper in front of her. "Bluebell, stop that!" she hissed. "You're supposed to be making friends with her!"

"Oops! Sorry!" whispered Bluebell. "I'll try. It's just that she's so mean!"

"I said she would be, and you promised to keep your temper," Katie reminded her, before ducking behind the book again.

Soon it was time for the class to go to an assembly in the auditorium. While they were gone, Katie had a chance to practice her flying in the empty classroom. Under Daisy's guidance she tried a few leaps into

the air and some hovering. When she got the hang of that, she tried flying from desk to desk. Rosehip held her hand at first, then after a few tries, she felt brave enough to try it all on her own. Soon she was zooming around the classroom, making loops and doing cartwheels in the air with the others. "Wow! This is the best feeling ever!" she cried, her heart soaring.

Then they heard the piano strike up the school song and a booming voice bellowing out the wrong words, accompanied by the wrong tune — and very, VERY LOUDLY! They all looked at each other in horror. "Bluebell!" they gasped.

Katie groaned. "She'll really need to start fitting in soon," she said. "Or she'll never be able to make friends with Tiffany!"

Soon the class returned and Katie and the fairies took cover on the windowsill. A few moments later, the children were sitting cross-legged on the carpet at the front of the room, ready for their next lesson. Four little heads peeked around the side of the math book, all their fingers crossed, necks craning to spot Bluebell. But suddenly their friend's head appeared above them, leaning far out of the window, taking deep breaths!

"Bluebell!" Katie hissed, as they all ducked down. "You can't just —"

But just then Tiffany's whiney voice came from across the classroom. "Mrs. Borthwick, look what she's doing!" she wailed.

Everyone turned to stare and the room exploded with laughter.

"Bluebell, come and sit down at once!" bellowed Mrs. Borthwick.

"I only wanted some fresh air," Bluebell mumbled, her face red with embarrassment. Then she hurried to sit down on the carpet with everyone else.

Katie watched Mrs. Borthwick take what her mom called a "deep cleansing breath."

"Now, children, today we're going to talk about healthy eating," she began. "So, who has a favorite food?"

A few of the children put their hands up, but before Mrs. Borthwick could choose someone, Bluebell shouted out cheerfully, "*I* don't have one! I don't eat food! I live on love and laughter!"

Everyone burst out laughing again, and poor Bluebell looked startled.

Mrs. Borthwick frowned at her. "Could you put your hand up if you

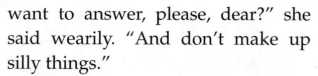

want to answer, please, dear?" she said wearily. "And don't make up silly things."

"But I'm not! It's true!" Bluebell insisted. Then she frowned and sulked at the unfairness of it all, and said nothing for the rest of the lesson. She even seemed to forget her task, and didn't smile at Tiffany once!

Peeking over the math book, Katie grimaced — this was not going as well as she'd hoped. In fact it was not going well *at all*.

"*I* could have done far better than her," Rosehip whispered, with satisfaction.

"I'm just glad it's not me out there," said Snowdrop, shuddering.

"Maybe I should have persuaded her not to do it," added Daisy, frowning.

"No, it's *my* fault," Katie insisted.

"I should have told her more about humans, and how to behave at school."

At recess, and after several more problems, Bluebell dragged herself across the playground and sat alone on a secluded bench. Checking that the coast was clear, Katie and the other fairies flew over to join her. As Daisy, Snowdrop, and

Rosehip flew around the bench playing tag, Katie tried to give Bluebell some emergency training on how to behave at school. "Just try to remember about putting your hand up and not shouting out," she advised, "and do your best to think of human answers to questions instead of fairy ones, and most importantly of all — don't stick your head out of the window!"

Katie thought Bluebell would laugh at this last thing, but she just looked even more upset. "I'm trying really hard," she wailed. "I just don't seem to

42

be getting anything right. Tiffany already thinks I'm awful. She won't tell me anything at this rate! Oh, maybe this isn't going to work after all!" And with that she settled into such a bad mood that it took two of Daisy's best jokes and one of Rosehip's liveliest fairy songs to cheer her up enough to keep on trying.

Luckily, after recess it was time for gym, which is the same in Fairyland as it is in the human world. Well, nearly the same.... When Mrs. Borthwick asked if Bluebell had gym clothes to change into, she just blinked at her and said that she'd never heard of such a thing, and she'd be staying in her blue skirt, which she'd never ever taken off, not even once!

Mrs. Borthwick sighed and told

her that it really wasn't nice to lie, and of course Bluebell insisted once again that she was telling the truth.

Peering down through a high window, Katie groaned — the emergency training hadn't sunk in at all!

But Mrs. Borthwick didn't stay annoyed with Bluebell for long. Soon the children were in the gym. Mrs. Borthwick picked a boy to be "it" first, and all the students played a big game of tag. Bluebell was great. The fairies had flown in through the window, and now Katie cringed behind the curtain, waiting for Bluebell to insist that she'd learned it all at fairy school. But when Mrs. Borthwick said "Well done," luckily she just replied, "Thank you."

Katie breathed a sigh of relief — maybe Bluebell was getting the hang of school after all!

As the class continued, Katie and the fairies peeked longingly from behind the curtain, tapping their feet.

"I wish *we* could play," said Snowdrop wistfully.

"Me, too," grumbled Rosehip, "I love tag! Look! Bluebell missed that girl. I'd be much better at this!"

"Rosehip, try not to be so jealous," said Daisy gently. "We have to support our friend."

Katie knew that Daisy was desperate to zoom into the center of the room and join in herself, and thought she was very kind for still thinking of Bluebell first. Then she suddenly remembered the task at hand and, when Bluebell ran close to them, she called out, "Psst! Try to get closer to Tiffany!"

Bluebell heard her and gave her a quick wink and a smile.

Just then Mrs. Borthwick told the class to find partners for playing catch. Bluebell immediately marched across the room and pushed another girl out of the way so she could stand next to Tiffany!

"Oh, no! I didn't mean like that!" Katie cried in despair. "And she was doing so well!"

Mrs. Borthwick wasn't happy either and made Bluebell sit out, in trouble again. The next time Tiffany came near Bluebell, she gave her a nasty look and hissed, "Stay away from me! You're a weird girl and your hair is stupid, so there!" She had such a mean look in her eyes that even brave Bluebell looked upset.

When everyone was busy playing catch with their partners, Katie and the fairies fluttered down

from the windowsill and landed in Bluebell's lap.

Rosehip was about to gloat, but the tear rolling down Bluebell's cheek stopped her.

"Oh, I really wanted to do well!" she sniffled, big fat tears plopping onto her friends' heads. "But I'm just messing everything up. I keep getting into trouble and Tiffany hates me. School is definitely not as much fun as I imagined!"

They all hugged her waist and, had anyone looked her way at that moment, they'd have thought she was wearing a fluttering, shimmering belt!

"Don't worry," said Katie kindly. "It'll work out, somehow."

At the end of gym class, Katie and the fairies hurried back to the windowsill. All the children lined up,

then Mrs. Borthwick led them back to the locker rooms to get ready for lunch. Bluebell dragged herself from the bench miserably, and stomped off to join the end of the line.

Chapter 4

After lunch, Bluebell wandered over to the far end of the school yard and found a lovely beech tree to sit under. Her friends soon spotted her and flew over. Bluebell looked a lot more cheerful, so they all crowded around, hoping she'd managed to make friends with Tiffany in the cafeteria.

"So, what did you find out?" asked Daisy, eagerly.

"Well, I found out that human food

is absolutely yummy!" Bluebell giggled. "Oh, you just wouldn't believe it. The taste! There was a burger with cheese that just melted in my mouth, and —"

"Well, if you think school lunches are nice, wait until you try chocolate ice cream, my mom's homemade pizza, or fat green grapes!" Katie said, grinning.

Rosehip shook her long flame-bright hair angrily.

"Fairies shouldn't eat human food," she announced. "You'll probably get sick soon." Katie noticed that she looked quite cheerful at the thought. Bluebell stuck her tongue out

at her. One of their famous arguments seemed to be brewing,
so Katie said quickly,
"Any luck with Tiffany?"

Bluebell shook her head
sadly. "She sat at another
table with her mean
friends and whispered
and pointed at me all
through lunch. It spoiled my chocolate chip cookies," she muttered, tears
in her eyes.

They all looked disap-
pointed, and Snowdrop
began to cry.

Katie put her arm
around her. "Shush, it's
OK," she said gently.

"But what if it's
not?" sobbed Snowdrop.
"What if the bulldozers
come tomorrow? We're not

ready to work the magic. We've only got one birth-stone so far, and even when we've collected them all, how will we know what to do with them?"

A thick gloom descended on the little group of friends. Snowdrop had said the very things out loud that they were all secretly frightened about.

"Even if we can't find out who's behind this, we need to keep collecting the birthstones, like the Fairy Queen told us," said Rosehip finally, breaking the silence. "We must be on red alert at all times for chances to find them."

Her friends all nodded in agreement.

"Good thinking, Rosehip," said Katie, who knew it was important to think positively, even when things looked really bad.

Just then the bell rang. Katie looked at Bluebell but she didn't move. "Bluebell, you have to go and line up," she told her.

"No way!" cried Bluebell, stamping her foot. "Tiffany hates me — she'll never tell me anything now! I don't want to spend even one more second with her, and I can't stand her calling me any more names!"

"But it's arts and crafts next," Katie told her. "And we're using beads. I just wonder if, maybe —"

"We might find another birth-stone there!" Rosehip interrupted gleefully.

"Yes!" cried Daisy. "The Fairy Queen works in mysterious ways. *We* think we're only at school to find out information from Tiffany, but maybe Her Eternal Majesty has led us here to find another birthstone as well!"

They all felt a lot more cheerful after that.

Bluebell leaped up. "Right! I'll see if I can spot any birthstones in arts and crafts. Then we can check the locker room after that, and the class-room after school, too. You never know, maybe we'll find one!"

"Good luck!" they chorused, and with that she marched off across the school yard to go line up.

"And try to remember what I taught you about school!" Katie called after her.

Bluebell turned and grinned at them. "Don't worry, it's all in here," she said, tapping her head.

"I really hope it is!" Katie muttered to herself.

When everyone had gone in, Katie and the fairies flew into the air, spinning and whirl-ing and whooping with joy. Even though things weren't going very well, nothing could take away the thrill of flying! Rosehip showed Katie how to flutter up to a small branch, flip into a half somersault,

and hang by her knees, and then they all tried it together, like a gymnastics team. After that, they got so carried away with playing tag in the air that they almost forgot to go and see how Bluebell was getting on in arts and crafts.

Katie led them back across the field to the school, doing somersaults all the way, and soon they were at the art room window. Daisy, Rosehip, and

Snowdrop touched down with grace and ease, whereas Katie crashed straight into the windowpane and fell to the ground. The other fairies swooped down to help her up. "Um, that's something we should have mentioned." Snowdrop said, giggling. "Landings take a bit of practice!"

Grinning, Katie dusted herself off, and they fluttered carefully back up into the air and through the open window. The children were all quietly working on their projects, heads down, and quiet chatter filled the room. The four friends needed to find a hiding place — and quickly, before anyone spotted them!

Chapter 5

Katie and the fairies dived down to the artroom floor, then inched along the baseboard and fluttered up to the sink. There they took cover under a pile of paint-smeared trays that sat waiting to be washed. They blended in so well with all the brightly-colored paint, it was like camouflage. Then they spotted Bluebell, sitting next to one of the nice girls in Katie's class (definitely not Tiffany!). She was

cheerfully threading beads onto a
string.

Katie watched as the children
picked beads out from bowls in the
center of each table. Some were
making necklaces, others worked on
beaded belts or bracelets, and a few
stuck the beads onto cardboard to
make pictures. "This is just the right
place to find another birthstone,"
she whispered to her friends. "Not

a really valuable one like an emerald or sapphire, of course, but the kind they make into beads — amethyst maybe, or even topaz!"

Bluebell was frantically hunting in the bowls and Katie knew that she was trying to find a birthstone. She just hoped that she'd remember how to behave — if she was accidentally naughty and got kicked out of arts and crafts it would be a disaster!

"Oh, those necklaces look so beautiful!" whispered Rosehip. "It's so unfair! *I* want to make one!"

"Me, too," said Snowdrop sadly.

They waved and waved from the sink until Bluebell finally noticed them.

She got up and went right over to Mrs. Borthwick, then stuck her hand in the air.

"Well, at least she's getting the hang

of putting her hand up," said Katie. "Sort of!"

"Yes, dear?" said Mrs. Borthwick, smiling kindly.

"May I wash my hands, please?" Bluebell asked politely.

"Certainly, dear," said Mrs. Borthwick, looking pleased with her at last.

When she came over to the sink, Daisy whispered, "Any luck?"

"Before you came in, I asked Mrs. Borthwick where all the beads came from. She said that they're mostly plastic, but that there are a few from some old broken necklaces," Bluebell said excitedly. "She couldn't quite remember, but she thought one of them might have been topaz, which is . . ."

"One of the birthstones!" finished Snowdrop.

"Good job, Bluebell," whispered Katie. "And keep looking! There's not much time!"

Bluebell nodded and hurried back to her seat. She kept on rummaging in the bowls on her table, but still didn't have any luck. She had to keep threading other beads onto her necklace, too, so that Mrs. Borthwick didn't start wondering what she was up to.

Katie wished she could help, but with so many children around, they couldn't risk being seen. She glanced up at the wall clock — there were only ten minutes left of the class now. Bluebell went over to the other tables, and soon she was searching in *their* bowls, too, but she still couldn't find a birthstone.

"Hurry, Bluebell, there's not much time!" Daisy hissed, but Bluebell

didn't hear her over the voices of the other children.

"I bet I could find that bead!" said Rosehip. "It's so unfair. She gets to do everything and she can't even do it right!"

Mrs. Borthwick was strolling around the class looking at everyone's work, and after a while she paused behind Bluebell. "May I?" she asked. Then, when Bluebell nodded, she held up her necklace. "Just stop for a moment and look at this, everyone," she said. "See how Bluebell has matched the colors so beautifully and come up with the idea of knotting the thread in places so that she ends up with clusters of three beads." There was a murmur of approval from the class. "It really is wonderful," Mrs. Borthwick added, handing back

the necklace with care. "You're very talented at arts and crafts, dear."

Bluebell was absolutely glowing with happiness at the praise, but it was the last straw for Rosehip. With fury in her eyes she launched herself across the room and knocked over all the bowls in front of Bluebell, sending beads flying everywhere! Everyone gasped — she'd been so quick it seemed as if *Bluebell* had done it.

Katie gasped — poor Bluebell. She'd be in trouble again, and just when Mrs. Borthwick was saying such nice things about her work, too!

"Bluebell, I am absolutely..." began Mrs. Borthwick, in her I've-had-it-up-to-here voice.

But Bluebell wasn't listening. *She* had seen the culprit. She leaped up and marched over to the sink, fists clenched, as the astonished class looked on. "How could you do that when I was finally doing well?" she shouted, seemingly at thin air. "You're just *jealous*!"

Rosehip stuck out her tongue at Bluebell and hid down between the paint trays. For a moment Bluebell seemed to forget that she was big and couldn't follow — she threw herself at the stack of trays, sending them crashing to the floor, flinging leftover paint everywhere.

Clinging to a tray, Rosehip went tumbling through the air, then she let

it go and dived into a
stack of paintings
piled on a stool.

"Come out,
Rosehip!" Bluebell
bellowed,
stamping
her foot.

As all eyes
were on Bluebell and
her strange behavior,
Katie was the only one
who noticed Snowdrop fly
into the air and zoom across the
room. But by the time she'd started
to ask her where she was going, she
was already gone.

But Katie soon forgot to wonder
about Snowdrop. She was too busy
gaping at Bluebell, who had snatched
up the paintings and was hurling each

one to the floor as she searched for Rosehip. They caught in the breeze from the open window and flipped and blew around the room.

Bluebell hardly noticed. "Where are you?" she shouted, spinning around to search the air. "You'll be sorry you messed with me, Rosehip!"

Snowdrop touched down beside Katie again and that was when Mrs. Borthwick absolutely bellowed, "Bluebell, stop that NOW!"

It was so loud that Bluebell jumped and instantly froze.

"Bluebell, I am so disappointed in you!" the red-faced teacher continued. "Clean up those paintings IMMEDIATELY and then put all those beads back into the bowls. How DARE you behave like this in my classroom, young lady!"

Bluebell hung her head and quietly

started picking up the paintings. Katie saw a tear plop onto the one on top.

Once everyone turned away and got back to their work, Rosehip fluttered up from her hiding place and touched down on the sink again. The others glared at her.

"I didn't mean to get Bluebell into so much trouble," she said sadly. "I just got really jealous and I couldn't help myself. I'm sorry."

"Now there's even less time to find the topaz," said Daisy reproachfully. But Rosehip looked so sorry that they couldn't stay angry with her for long.

"Sorry, Bluebell," Rosehip whispered, but she didn't seem to hear.

When she'd picked up the paintings, Bluebell went and put the beads away, still trying to look carefully at each one. But soon Mrs. Borthwick told them all to clean up because it was time to go home, and Bluebell had no choice but to shovel handfuls of beads back into the bowls. Her eyes scanned the piles of beads desperately, but she couldn't see a topaz one anywhere.

All the fairies looked as utterly miserable as Katie felt. This had been the perfect chance to get another birthstone and they'd missed it.

Finally, Mrs. Borthwick clapped her hands and everyone clapped back. "Well, seeing as Bluebell's only with us today," she said, "she may take her necklace home. But the rest of

us are going to display ours, so please hand them in to me." One of the boys tried to sneak his belt into his bag. "That includes you," she told him sternly.

Katie watched Bluebell tying her beautiful necklace around her neck, but there was no happiness on her face. She felt so sorry for her — poor Bluebell had been so brave when she'd volunteered to turn big. It should have been fun, but instead everything had gone wrong. She hadn't gotten any information from Tiffany, or found a topaz bead, and she'd been in trouble all day!

Chapter 6

As everyone headed out to the playground to meet their parents, the five friends took a detour into the locker room. Bluebell slumped miserably on a bench and the others fluttered down to sit beside her.

"Oh, I'm so sorry, I completely failed!" wailed Bluebell.

They were all comforting her when suddenly the locker room door swung open. Katie and the fairies all dived

for cover behind Bluebell as someone came in.

It was absolutely the last person they were expecting to see.

It was Tiffany!

For a moment, Bluebell looked frightened, wondering what mean thing she would say or do next. But then she managed to put on a bored expression. "What do you want?" she asked, sulkily.

"I wanted to say I'm sorry about being mean to you before," said Tiffany.

Bluebell blinked at her in disbelief.

"I like you now," she continued, sitting down next to Bluebell on the bench. "I realized that you like trouble just like me. It was so funny when you talked back to Mrs. Borthwick in the healthy-food lesson, and

when you lied about your hair, and when you sang really loud at the assembly on purpose to be rude. But best of all was when you wrecked the art room. That was great!"

"I didn't mean . . ." Bluebell began, but Katie nudged her hard in the back. "Uh, yes, getting into trouble is fun," she said instead, seeing her chance to make friends with Tiffany.

"It is, isn't it?" said Tiffany gleefully. "But . . . you don't actually *like* that awful Katie girl, do you?"

Katie could see Bluebell's fists tightening in anger at this, but then she seemed to remember her mission and smiled. "Uh, well, I don't really know her. It's just because my family might move here that I'm visiting your lovely, uh, I mean, this yucky dump," Bluebell babbled. "I've never even met Katie."

"You wouldn't want to, she's so boring!" exclaimed Tiffany; then she added, "Is it really true what you said about flying to school?"

"Uh, yes, because, uh . . ." Bluebell paused to think of a human-sounding answer, as Katie had taught her. "Because my dad's very rich; he's got a helichopper," she finished.

Katie cringed but Tiffany didn't seem suspicious. "Helicopter," she corrected, looking impressed.

Bluebell saw her chance, took a deep breath, and said, "Uh, speaking of dads, your dad's Max Towner, isn't he? Someone told me that he built those houses on the edge of town."

The fairies all smiled excitedly at one another as Tiffany puffed up with pride.

"Yes, he did," she replied. "He's building a lot more, too. There's a piece of land with a stupid old oak tree on it, and he's going to build a mansion there. If I throw a big enough tantrum, I bet he'll let me sit in the bulldozer and do the job, too! I can't wait to see that old hunk of wood come crashing down!"

Bluebell gasped in horror, then quickly turned it into a pretend yelp

of excitement. "And when will this happen?" she managed to ask.

"I don't know," said Tiffany. "Daddy says the exact date has to be Top Secret in case some stupid tree lovers find out about it and start a protest."

"Oh, right," said Bluebell.

"Anyway, I have to go," said Tiffany. "I'm going shopping — Mom's buying me a new dress, well, probably two."

"Um, yes, right — I have to go and buy some new dresses, too," said Bluebell uncertainly. "But first I have to change. See you later."

Of course, Tiffany didn't realize that she meant change back into a fairy! With a big smile at Bluebell and an invitation to come back any time, she left.

When the door had swung shut

again, Katie and the fairies came out and leaped on to Bluebell's lap.

"Good job, Bluebell!" Snowdrop squealed. "Now we know for sure that Max Towner is the culprit!"

"We just have to find out when he's planning to knock down the tree!" cried Rosehip.

"We're so proud of you, Bluebell," added Daisy.

Bluebell couldn't help smiling. She was very proud of herself, too! "We didn't find the topaz, though," she said with a sigh.

"Yes, we did," said Snowdrop. She spoke so softly that no one paid any attention at first. "We got it," she repeated, louder, and they all turned to gape at her.

Smiling, she reached into the pocket of her purple petal skirt and pulled out a smooth shiny brown bead.

Daisy, Rosehip, and Katie leaped on her, hugging her tight! "Oh, Snowdrop! Good job!" cried Bluebell.

"But how?" asked Daisy when they broke apart.

"And when?" said Rosehip.

"When Bluebell was making a scene by the sink trying to get ahold of you, everyone was so distracted that I knew I could fly over and search the beads on the floor," Snowdrop explained.

Katie grinned. "So that's what you were up to!"

Snowdrop smiled shyly. "I spotted

this and it looked the right color for topaz, so I grabbed it," she said. "I suppose it was lucky that Rosehip and Bluebell were fighting after all!"

"But we weren't really!" Rosehip told Snowdrop. "I guessed that you were planning to search for a bead, that's why I created a diversion!"

"And I pretended to get really mad at Rosehip so that everyone would look at me, to give you time to get across the room and grab the bead!" Bluebell insisted.

They gave each other a hug as if to prove it.

Katie stifled a giggle and Daisy raised her eyebrows. "Of course you did," she said. "Whatever you say."

"Now, we have to change back quickly, my mom will be waiting," said Katie. She felt sad about losing her beautiful shimmering fairy

wings, of course, but the thought of her mom waiting in the playground for her more than made up for it.

Bluebell lay down on the bench, and once Snowdrop had sprinkled Katie's and Bluebell's palms with fairy dust, they pressed them tightly together.

This time, Katie was expecting the lightning zap, but it still startled her. Then a loud POP! brought her back to her normal size. She shook her arms and legs, while a fairy-sized Bluebell fluttered her wings and did a few happy fairy hops. "It's nice to be me again!" they both said at once, making everyone laugh.

"Oh, no!" cried Katie, pointing at Bluebell's neck. "You should have taken off my tie — how on earth am I going to explain that to my mom?"

They all laughed again as Bluebell

handed Katie the teeny-weeny tie, which she put around her wrist like a bracelet.

Then Katie hurried out into the playground, with the fairies stowed safely in her book bag. After the biggest hug, she pulled her mom away quickly before anyone from her class could see her and wonder what she was doing there! On the way home, Katie's mom asked her what she did that day. Katie smiled a mysterious smile and said, "Well, we were dancing in music and it felt like I was flying."

Katie's mom squeezed her hand. "I've always wanted to fly," she said dreamily. "Can you imagine it, darling? Soaring and twirling and dancing in the air? Wouldn't it be wonderful?"

"Just wonderful," Katie repeated, smiling secretly to herself.

As soon as she got home, Katie ran upstairs to hide the topaz bead safely away in her jewelry box with the garnet ring. Only ten more birthstones to find and they'd be able to save the tree!

Then, after a snack of apple juice  and carrot cake with her mom (missing lunch had left her very hungry!), she hurried out to the Fairy House. Once Katie had shrunk down to

fairy size (no wings this time, though!), she went inside. But no one ran to greet her. "Anyone home?" she called. Still nothing. Then she heard some muffled giggling and a voice called down the stairs, "Hide and seek! You're it!"

Katie grinned and stomped up the stairs, calling, "I'm coming to get you!" It didn't take her long to find the fairies, since they were no good at keeping still *or* being quiet!

Soon she'd pulled Bluebell out of the empty bathtub, gotten Snowdrop out of her wardrobe, discovered Rosehip under her bed, and found Daisy squashed into a kitchen cupboard!

After a few more games, they all lay in a line on Bluebell's polka-dot bedspread, their heads dangling over the edge.

"I wish *I* could have been big!" said Daisy, with a sigh. "I didn't say so before because I didn't want to make any problems, but it looked like so much fun — especially the art and gym classes!"

"I think we all wish we could have done that!" said Snowdrop, sadly.

"I know. We can have our own class, right here!" cried Rosehip.

"What a great idea!" Bluebell giggled. "And this time I won't get in trouble and have to sit it out!"

"You might!" said Rosehip with a laugh.

"I won't!" countered Bluebell. "Because *this time* I'm going to be the teacher, and I won't get *myself* in trouble, so there!"

Laughing, they pulled each other into the living room and pushed the rose-petal sofas and dandelion rugs

against the walls. Then Rosehip played the enchanted piano, and Bluebell pretended to be the teacher, and the fairies and Katie started singing and laughing while they skipped and whirled and twirled until it was time for dinner.

The End

Bluebell
Spring fairy

Likes:

blue, blue, blue, and more blue,
doing somersaults in the air, dancing

Dislikes:

finishing second, being told what to do

Daisy
Summer fairy

Likes:

everyone to be friends, bright sunshine,
cheery yellow colors, smiling

Dislikes:

arguments, cold dark places,
ugly orange dresses

Rosehip
Autumn fairy

Likes:

riding magic ponies, telling Bluebell
what to do, playing the piano, singing

Dislikes:

keeping quiet, boring colors,
not being the center of attention!

Snowdrop
Winter fairy

Likes:

singing fairy songs, cool quiet places, riding her
favorite magical unicorn, making snowfairies

Dislikes:

being too hot, keeping secrets

Don't miss book three!

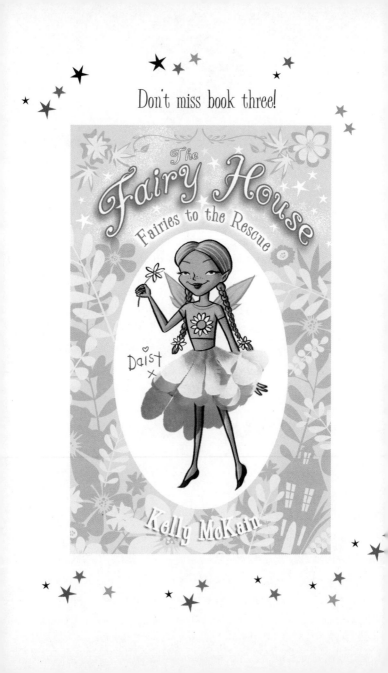

The Fairy House

Fairies to the Rescue

Daist
x

Kelly McKain